ANIMAL
✛RESCUE CENTER

The
Sad
Pony

ANIMAL MAGIC

This series is for my riding friend Shelley,
who cares about all animals.

Other titles in the series:

The Unwanted Puppy

The Home-alone Kitten

The Injured Fox Kit

The Homeless Foal

The Runaway Rabbit

The Lost Duckling

The Abandoned Hamster

The Porch Puppy

tiger tales

5 River Road, Suite 128, Wilton, CT 06897
Published in the United States 2018
Originally published in Great Britain 2009
as *The Problem Pony* by the Little Tiger Group
Text copyright © 2009, 2018 Jenny Oldfield
Interior illustrations copyright © 2018 Artful Doodlers
Cover illustration copyright © 2018 Anna Chernyshova
Images courtesy of www.shutterstock.com
ISBN-13: 978-1-68010-427-1
ISBN-10: 1-68010-427-6
Printed in China
STP/1800/0189/0218

For more insight and activities, visit us at www.tigertalesbooks.com

Contents

ANIMAL MAGIC
RESCUE CENTER

🏠 HOME

😺 ADOPT

✋ FRIENDS

MEET THE ANIMALS IN NEED OF A HOME!

TIGER

Meet Tiger. He's young and very affectionate, waiting patiently for that special person to give him the love he needs.

PRINCE

There's a lot of bull mastiff in Prince, but we can't say exactly how old he is or where he came from. Will need a lot of TLC.

DOTTY

A little sweetie who's been living rough. She's looking forward to finding a loving new owner.

SITE SEARCH

NEWS

HELP US

CONTACT

DONATE!

SMOKEY

Silky, soft, and very hard to say no to, handsome Smokey is neutered and house-trained, too!

TUCKER

A beautiful short-haired collie-cross who loves to play. Lively Tucker needs plenty of walks!

TOFFEE AND FUDGE

This adorable pair is friendly and like being picked up. Can you give them a home together?

Chapter One

A New Year's Surprise!

"'Bye, Mom! 'Bye, Dad!" Ella Harrison stood outside the security checkpoint in the airport terminal, waving as her parents disappeared down the hallway to their departure gate.

"Don't forget—take lots of pictures of you swimming with dolphins!" Ella's brother, Caleb, called after them.

"Watch out for alligators!" Ella's voice was drowned out by an airport announcement.

The Sad Pony

Caleb and Ella's grandfather, Jimmy Harrison, waited until Mom and Dad were out of sight, then took over. "Come on, Ella, time to go." He led her and Caleb back through the terminal and out to the parking lot. "Don't worry about them," he smiled. "They're going to have a fantastic time in Florida. And this vacation is your dad's surprise late Christmas present to your mom, so they're bound to have fun."

Ella nodded as she climbed into the truck. "I know, Grandpa. I'm really glad they're going on vacation, but I'm still going to miss them."

"Well, we'll be so busy at Animal Magic that you won't have time to feel sad," Caleb warned. "We won't have a spare second to think about them sunning themselves on a beach with palm trees, looking out at a blue sea, snorkeling, swimming with dolphins…."

"Stop, you're making me jealous!" Ella put her hands over her ears. It was Friday—New Year's Eve—and the snow that had fallen over Christmas had long since melted. Now everything was gray and damp, the clouds were heavy, and the days short. Ella sighed, then stared out the window at the wet city streets.

"Cheer up, Ella," Grandpa said, grinning. "I happen to know that, besides arranging emergency vet coverage while they're away, your mom and dad have lined up a nice surprise for you and Caleb later today."

Caleb leaned forward from the back seat. "What kind of surprise?"

"If I told you now, it wouldn't be a surprise, would it?" their grandpa laughed.

"Tell us anyway," Ella begged. She was thinking that it might be a trip to the movies or a visit to their favorite pizza restaurant.

"No, I'm sworn to secrecy!" Leaving the city behind, Grandpa followed signs for the highway, then took the exit marked Crystal Park. Pretty soon, they were driving through farmland and heading for home.

"Hey, Caleb, I'm glad you're back. I was hoping you'd feed the cats," Jen said the minute he walked into the reception area at Animal Magic. Jen, the center's veterinary assistant, was filling in for Mom and Dad while they were on vacation, and she seemed really busy already.

"No problem," Caleb said, hurrying down the hallway to the storage room.

"And Ella, could you come and help me with Tiger?"

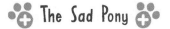

Ella waved good-bye to her grandpa, then followed Jen into an examination room where she saw a pet carrier on the table. Inside the carrier was a sad-looking orange tabby cat, half covered by a dirty fleece blanket.

"Tiger's owner dropped him off half an hour ago," Jen explained. She put on a pair of surgical gloves and dumped the blanket in the garbage can before lifting the cat out of the carrier and placing him carefully on the scrubbed, shiny table. "She wasn't very happy with you, was she? You poor thing."

Ella noticed that the little cat looked miserable. "Why, what did he do?"

"It's not something he did, actually." Carefully, Jen opened Tiger's mouth and peered inside, then examined his eyes.

"He's covered in fleas, poor little guy, and his owner is complaining that she's developed a skin condition called flea allergy dermatitis."

"So she left him with us?" Ella checked. She was feeling more and more sorry for the shivering cat.

Jen nodded. "She said there was no chance of her taking him back, so I promised we'd find a home for him once we've dealt with the fleas."

"How come the owner didn't treat them herself?"

"I have no idea," Jen answered. "It doesn't look like she even bothered to wash his bedding, judging by the looks of that blanket. Uh-oh, Ella, I wouldn't pet Tiger if I were you—not yet."

Ella stepped back. "We'll take a picture, and Caleb can put him on the website right away," she decided. "What Tiger needs is someone who gives him regular flea treatments, plus lots of cuddles!"

"Exactly," Jen agreed. She returned the patient to the carrier and prepared to carry him into the quarantine section of the cat area. "I did get one good piece of news while you were at the airport."

Ella followed her down the hallway. "What is it?"

"Some people saw Tucker on the

website—they want to come in and take a look at him."

Tucker was a handsome, short-haired collie-cross who had been at Animal Magic since long before Christmas. "Did they sound nice?" Ella asked.

"Yes, very," Jen replied, stepping aside to let Caleb hurry ahead to the cat area with two dishes of cat food. "Caleb, I was telling Ella—we've got someone interested in adopting Tucker."

"Cool!" Caleb had a soft spot for the collie-cross, who was playful and full of energy. "When are they coming in?"

"Tomorrow's Saturday, isn't it? So, tomorrow at two o'clock. Their names are Jane and Rob Goodspeed. I wrote the appointment in the book."

"Okay. But right now we have to

make sure we feed Tiger," Ella told
Caleb as Jen put the new arrival in
isolation at the end of the row of cats
all needing good homes. She paused by
Dottie the stray cat's cage and
peered in. "You're looking
good," she said, smiling
as Dottie purred,
then dug into her
meal. Then Ella
ran after Jen,
who had gone
into the small
animals' unit.

"Meet another
new arrival." Jen
lifted a gray and
white rabbit out
of a cage.

"He's cute!" Ella rubbed the silky fur. "What's his name?"

"This is Smokey. He's an unwanted Christmas present."

"Oh—you're beautiful!" Ella assured him as she took him from Jen. She liked the way he twitched his ears and wrinkled his nose at the same time. "Don't worry—someone will give you a great new home."

"After we've neutered you and given you a thorough health check," Jen added. "By the way, I haven't had time to ask—did your mom and dad get on their way safely?"

Ella cuddled Smokey and nodded. "They're in the air right now, lucky ducks."

Jen petted the rabbit, then helped Ella

put him back in his cage. Then they
hurried back into the reception area.

"What I don't get is why they left you
all by yourself." Ella had been puzzled
by this. It wasn't like her mom to push a
lot of responsibility on to her assistant.

"I'm not by myself—I've got you and
Caleb." Looking mysterious, Jen began
to straighten some paperwork on the
desk. "And you're still on vacation from
school, so I'm sure we'll do just fine."

Ella nodded. If every day was as busy
as today, she wasn't sure they would.
But she didn't say anything to Jen.
Instead, she went to hang some new
notices on the board by the window.

"Jen, is it okay if I go to the house
and check on Holly?" she asked when
she'd finished.

"Sure. I'm surprised you lasted this long!" Jen smiled as Ella darted off.

Holly was the adorable new addition to the Harrison family—a black-and-white Border collie puppy who'd come to them on Christmas Eve. In one week she'd made herself completely at home in the kitchen of the old farmhouse. She had her own bed by the side of the fireplace, her favorite spot under the table, and a habit of jumping up into the lap of whoever came in for coffee.

"Holly, where are you?" Ella cried as she ran into the kitchen.

"She's in here," Caleb called from the living room. He'd finished feeding the cats and beaten Ella to it.

Ella hurried into the hallway. "Hey, Holly, it's me!"

The puppy scrambled to meet her, jumping up and yelping with joy.

"Down, Holly!" Ella ordered, trying not to burst into delighted laughter.

The excited puppy jumped up again. Then she squirmed on the floor, leaving a small puddle on the tiles.

"Uh-oh, the dreaded excitement accident!" Grinning, Ella went back into the kitchen for the mop. Holly saw it and pounced. "No, Holly. This is a mop, not something to play with!" She was still dealing with the puddle when Caleb appeared.

"Hey, Ella, come in here," he said with a mysterious smile.

"What's the big secret?" Ella put down the mop and went into the living room—to find Joel standing there.

❄️ A New Year's Surprise! ❄️

"Hello, Ella."

"Joel!" She ran to hug the young veterinary assistant who had left Animal Magic a few months earlier to go and work in Australia. "Why? I mean, what are…?" Ella paused mid-sentence. "Hey, are you our surprise?"

Joel gave her a wide grin. "Yes! I'm home for the New Year."

"Wow!" Ella was speechless. She'd missed seeing Joel's kind, smiling face around the place and his beat-up car parked in the yard. "Happy New Year! Cool surprise!"

"It gets better," Caleb promised, scooping Holly up as she ran between his legs. "Tell her, Joel."

"I'm here for a couple of weeks, and I told your mom that instead of just sitting around twiddling my thumbs, I'd help out here."

"At Animal Magic?" Ella gasped.

"Where else?" Joel grinned. "In fact, I'm off to help Jen."

"Right now?" Ella gasped.

"Right this very minute." Joel laughed as he walked out of the house and across the yard.

Chapter Two

A Home for Tucker

"Happy New Year!" Annie Brooks greeted Ella from Rosie's stable.

It was Saturday, and Ella had gotten up early to bring Annie the surprise news about Joel.

"Yeah, Happy New Year!" she gasped now, grinning at Annie and seizing a mucking-out fork. "It definitely is a happy, Happy New Year!"

"Why? What happened?" Annie asked as Rosie, the Shetland pony, gave

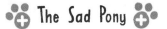

her a nudge in the back, then barged past to stick her shaggy head over the door.

"Hi, Rosie." Ella grinned. She rubbed the pony's nose. "Joel has come back to help out at Animal Magic!"

"Hey, cool! How long is he staying?"

The two girls chatted as Ella got roped into mucking out Buttercup and Chance's stable. "Until Mom and Dad get back. Jen says she's glad to have help, and of course Joel already knows everything about the rescue center. Hey, are you going to keep the horses in today or turn them out into the field?"

Annie glanced up at the blue sky. "Mom said to let them out."

"It's cold," Ella warned. "There's ice on all the paths."

"Maybe we'll just leave them out for the morning, then bring them in again." Annie went to the tack room to grab the horses' rugs while Ella forked muck into a wheelbarrow.

"It's so cool—Joel's been telling us about working in Australia. He loves it."

"Here's Chance's rug," Annie interrupted. "Stand still, Rosie, while I put yours on."

Quickly, Ella slid the horse rug over young Chance's back and buckled the straps. She smiled to herself as she heard a scuffle.

"Stand still, Rosie. I can't do the straps if you dance around like that. That's better. No, I don't have any treats in my pocket—stop that, you naughty pony!"

By the time Annie had finished with Rosie, Ella had rugged Buttercup and let her and Chance out into the frosty field.

The gray mare and her foal trotted off down the slope. They'd spotted Caleb on the path and had gone to say hello.

"Hi, Caleb!" Ella waved and ran to join them. "What are you up to?"

"I'm taking Tucker for a walk before

the Goodspeeds come to see him,"
he explained. "And I brought Holly
along, too."

"Ahh!" Leaning over the fence, Ella
laughed to see little Holly on the end of
the leash. The puppy was sniffing the
long grass. Then she lifted her head to
shake off the white frost from the tip of
her black nose.

"Watch out! Here comes Rosie," Caleb
warned.

At last Annie had gotten Rosie's rug
on, and now the sturdy Shetland was
frisking down the slope.

"Wait for me!" Annie called, zipping
up her thick jacket and coming to join
Ella and Caleb.

"How's Rosie settling in?" Caleb asked
Annie. It was less than two weeks since

Rosie had moved in to the Brooks's new stables. Before that, the pony had stayed next door at Animal Magic, waiting for someone to adopt her.

"Good," Annie reported. "She still gets along well with Buttercup and Chance."

"Who's the boss out of the three of them?" Caleb asked. He let Tucker off the leash to run along the riverside path.

"Rosie!" Annie answered quickly. "She's the smallest, but she definitely orders the other two around."

As if to prove it, Rosie began to nudge and push at Chance as if she was rounding him up and herding him back up the hill.

Ella and Caleb laughed. "We miss her," Ella said.

"Mom says she's a little character."
Annie smiled. "Hey, what's she up to
now?"

Rosie had suddenly broken away from
Chance and was making a beeline for
the fence that separated the Brooks's
field from the yard at Animal Magic.
She covered the ground as fast as her
little legs would carry her.

"Rosie, stop!" Ella yelled. She chased
after the pony, trying to head her off
before she reached the boundary.

But Rosie wouldn't listen. She charged
straight at the high fence.

"Uh-oh, she's going to jump!" Caleb
cringed and closed his eyes. "I can't
look."

"She's too small! She'll never make it!"
Annie wailed.

Ella sprinted across the field and got to the fence seconds before Rosie. She stood in the pony's path, waving both arms above her head, warning her away.

At the last second, Rosie put on the brakes and slid to a stop along the frosty ground, digging up the turf just inches from the high fence.

"No way was that a good idea!" Ella told her sternly. "If you want to come and visit us, you have to be good and let Annie lead you through the gate."

Rosie snickered, then trotted up to Ella.

"Okay, so now you're sorry." Ella laughed, relenting and letting Rosie push her nose against her hand. "But just remember—this is your home now. So no more crazy ideas about getting back to Animal Magic!"

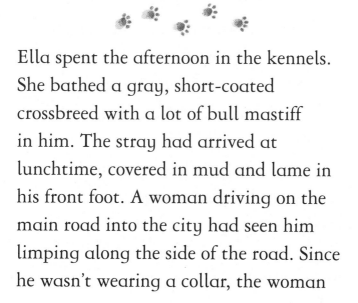

Ella spent the afternoon in the kennels. She bathed a gray, short-coated crossbreed with a lot of bull mastiff in him. The stray had arrived at lunchtime, covered in mud and lame in his front foot. A woman driving on the main road into the city had seen him limping along the side of the road. Since he wasn't wearing a collar, the woman had decided to bring him to the rescue center.

"If only people would microchip their pets," Jen sighed, watching Ella begin to clean up the dog. "We'll hold him for a while in case the owner comes looking, but my guess is that he'll end up on our website."

Ella sponged the dog down, then rubbed him dry with a towel. "Don't worry—I'm going to choose a name for you…. Let's call you Prince! And we'll find you a kind new owner," she promised.

Further down the row of kennels, Caleb was busy sprucing up Tucker, ready for his appointment with the Goodspeeds. "You're looking handsome," he said.

Just then, Joel poked his head around the door. "Ella, do you mind giving me a hand with two new arrivals?"

"No problem." Giving Prince one last rub, she put him safely back in his kennel and dashed to the reception area.

"Oh, and Caleb, the Goodspeeds are here," Joel added. "Bring Tucker out."

"It's your big moment," Caleb told Tucker, putting him on the leash and following Ella and Joel out of the kennels.

"Two more strays." Joel showed Ella the small cage on top of the reception desk. "Brought in by Pete Knight from Main Street. He found them hiding in his shed, searching for some warmth."

Curious, Ella peered into the cage to see two guinea pigs—one toffee colored, one brown and white. They were huddled in a corner, scratching at the floor of the cage with their pink front feet.

"Jen examined them and says they're both males. Would you like to choose names?" Joel asked Ella.

"Hmm…. How about Toffee and Fudge?" She grinned as the names popped into her head.

"Nice one. Toffee and Fudge it is. I'm sure they'll be snapped up the minute you put them on the website."

Ella nodded, and then she stepped aside to let Tucker make his big entrance with Caleb. There was a middle-aged man and a woman sitting in the waiting area, looking nervous but eager.

"This is Tucker," Caleb told the couple.

"Sit, Tucker!"

The obedient dog instantly followed his command.

"He's sweet," Mrs. Goodspeed said. "See his eyes—they look intelligent."

"He's very lively when you take him out for a walk," Caleb warned her.

"Will he come back when you call him?" Mr. Goodspeed asked.

Caleb nodded. "Would you like to come for a walk and see him in action?"

"Great idea," Mr. Goodspeed agreed. "We don't want to adopt him and then find out that he's too much for us to handle."

So while Caleb took Tucker and the Goodspeeds for a walk by the river, Ella helped Joel with Toffee and Fudge. "I'll take their picture for the website," she decided. "Joel, can you hold them, one in each hand? Look this way, you two. That's it—smile!"

"You know how to upload the picture, don't you?" Joel asked, taking a quick look at the result.

"Yes. Should I add their entry now?"

"Feel free," Joel said, hurrying on to his next job.

So Ella sat at the computer. She put
the cute picture onto the Animal Magic
website, then began to type. "Toffee and
Fudge." She stopped to compose the next
sentence, then began again. "Friendly
and like to be picked up." *Hmm, I should
mention how handsome and cuddly they are,*
she thought.

Before she could add anything else,
the phone rang, and Ella picked it up.
"Hello, this is Animal Magic."

"Hello, Animal Magic, this is Mark
Harrison!"

"Dad!" Ella gasped. "Where are you?"

"In Miami Beach, in the world's best
hotel," he said. "I'm sitting on a balcony
overlooking the ocean. It's magic."

"Have you seen any dolphins?" Ella
asked.

"Not yet. How are you, Ella? How's Caleb? Is he there?"

"No. He's out with Tucker. We think we've found him a home."

"Good, fingers crossed. Did you like our surprise?"

"You mean Joel? So cool!" Ella answered happily, smiling as Joel himself came across to take the phone.

"Listen, Mark, you're not allowed to ask any questions about work," he warned. "This is your vacation, remember?"

Seeing Caleb come back into the yard with Tucker and the Goodspeeds, Ella ran to open the door.

Mrs. Goodspeed led Tucker in on the leash. "Good boy, Tucker. Sit!"

He sat by her side, staring up at her

with his big, brown eyes.

"Well?" Ella asked.

"He's wonderful!" Mrs. Goodspeed sighed. "I can picture us taking him for walks in the woods behind our house, throwing a stick and getting him to fetch it."

"In other words, we'll take him," her husband said with a smile.

Tucker seemed to understand. He gave a yelp of pleasure, stood up, and wagged his tail to a bright new future with Mr. and Mrs. Goodspeed.

Chapter Three
The Accident

That night, Ella slept soundly and woke
early, well before she thought Caleb or
Jen would be up. She put on her robe
and crept downstairs into the kitchen to
spend one-on-one time with Holly.

"Hi!" she whispered.

The puppy was thrilled to see her. She
leaped from her basket and ran across
the kitchen floor toward Ella. Ella
picked her up and let her snuggle into
her arms.

"Shh! Don't wake the others," she whispered, tiptoeing into the living room.

"No need to whisper," Caleb grinned. "I'm already awake!"

Awake and watching TV, stretched out on the couch with a bowl of cereal resting on his chest. Ella stared in disbelief.

"No need to look like that. I've been up for a while. "

In the background, the music for
the start of the Tina Sanchez Show,
one of the morning talk shows, began,
and Tina appeared on-screen. She ran
through the items on the morning
program—an interview with a big
movie director, and the chance to enter
an exciting competition, but before that
a segment on a series of children's pony
books written by a famous actress.

"Boring!" Caleb sighed. He was about
to switch channels when Ella stopped
him.

"Leave it on. I want to see the part
about the pony books."

"I can't stand talk shows," Caleb said.
But he gave in, and they watched the
host introduce the celebrity at home on
her converted farm.

Ella sat cross-legged in front of the TV with Holly in her lap. "Look at the ponies, Holly!"

"It's no secret that I love horses," Tina went on, while the camera panned over a green field dotted with beautiful thoroughbreds. "But I still wonder what persuaded top actress Venus Hall to break into the world of pony books?"

The camera settled on a tall, slim figure dressed in jodhpurs and long black boots. "Ever since I was a little girl, I dreamed of having my own pony," Venus replied.

"Blah, blah!" Caleb snorted.

"So the books are a way of making your childhood dream come true?" Tina asked.

"Exactly." Venus nodded.

"Holly, sit!" Ella said as the puppy leaped off her lap and barked at the TV screen. She leaned forward to pick her up, but Holly darted around the back of the TV. "Watch out for the wires!" Ella cried. "Caleb, turn the TV off, quickly, so Holly won't get an electric shock!"

There was a scuffle behind the TV before Ella emerged triumphant. "I'll take Holly back into the kitchen—it's safer there," she decided.

"Good, now I can switch channels," Caleb grunted.

Back in the kitchen, the phone was ringing. It was Annie, wanting to know if Ella would like to ride Buttercup.

"When?" Ella asked.

"Now," Annie told her.

"Okay, I'll check with Jen."

Luckily, Jen had just come downstairs in her robe. Quickly, Ella asked permission, then spoke into the phone again. "Give me five minutes to get dressed," she said excitedly, "and I'll be right there!"

Out in the Brooks's field, Ella found that her friend had already saddled Buttercup but was struggling with the bridle.

"She keeps on raising her head so I can't reach her mouth," Annie complained.

In the stable next door, Rosie gave a shrill neigh and a hefty kick at the door.

"Hi, Rosie!" Ella replied cheerfully. She took the bridle from Annie and slipped the reins over Buttercup's head. "This should do the trick," she promised.

Sure enough, the horse felt the reins hanging loose around her neck and saw Ella waiting patiently with the bit in her hand. Obediently, she lowered her head and waited for Ella to slip the bit between her teeth.

Annie nodded. "Cool. Here's the hard hat. You take a turn first," she offered.

Ella put on the hat while Annie opened the stable door and stood back.

Another kick at her door told them Rosie wanted to come, too.

"Stay here, Rosie. We won't be long," Annie told the Shetland, giving her a quick pet.

"How long has she been kicking the door?" Ella asked as she put her feet in the stirrups and set off slowly down the field.

"For a couple of days. Oh, Mom wants us to stay in the field," Annie told Ella. "She says not to go above a trot."

So Ella rode steadily, letting Buttercup take her time. Back at the stable, naughty Rosie was still kicking

and banging, and the back door to
Annie's house had opened.

"Uh-oh, I bet Mom's mad," Annie
muttered, leaving Ella to ride and
jogging back up the hill. But before she
reached the stable, Rosie had landed an
extra-hard kick and forced the bolt. The
stable door flew open and the little pony
barged out in a bid for freedom.

"No, go back!" Annie yelled.

By now, Mrs. Brooks had come out into her yard and started to run down the path toward the field.

Taking no notice of Annie, Rosie tried the same trick as the day before. She galloped toward the fence, looking for all the world as if she was going to clear it and land in the yard at Animal Magic.

"Oh, no!" Annie wailed.

Her mom sprinted down the path.

"Come on, Buttercup, trot on!" Ella cried, urging the horse to catch up with Rosie. Buttercup's long legs quickly covered the ground. "Oh, no, you don't!" Ella shouted, getting into position to cut Rosie off again. Just in time, she got to the right spot and stood her ground.

Once more, the pony threatened to jump and stopped at the last second. She lowered her head so that her shaggy brown mane covered her eyes, then she glanced up playfully at Ella.

"It's not funny!" Ella sighed, signaling to Annie that everything was okay.

Annie waved back, then ran to tell her mom.

But it was her dad who greeted her

from the yard.

"Where's Mom?" Annie asked. The last she knew, her mom had been sprinting down the path to see what had caused the chaos in the field.

"Your mom fell," Mr. Brooks explained over the fence. "She slipped on the ice."

"Mom, are you all right?" Annie gasped, spotting her mom leaning heavily against a low wall.

Her dad shook his head. "She'll be okay, but I'm going to drive her to the hospital to get an X-ray of her leg. It'll be best if you stay with Ella."

"Can't I come?" Annie begged.

But her dad told her she had to stay. "I'll call you as soon as we have any news," he promised, rushing off to help Mrs. Brooks into the car.

By the time Ella had ridden up and slid down from the saddle, Annie was in tears.

"It's all Rosie's fault!" she cried. "Mom had an accident."

It took a while for Ella to understand, but when she did, she quickly unsaddled Buttercup and put her in the stable. In the background she heard the sound of Mr. Brooks's car driving out onto Main Street. "Wait here while I get Rosie back into her stable," she told Annie.

Soon all the horses were inside, and Ella took Annie back to her house. She led her into the kitchen, where Jen was cooking bacon. "Mrs. Brooks had an accident," she explained. "Rosie was trying to escape again. Mrs. Brooks tried to stop her, and she slipped on some ice. I'm not sure, but I think Rosie's limping, too."

Jen quickly took control. "Caleb, you can finish making your bacon and egg sandwich, can't you? I'm going to pop next door and take a look at Rosie. Ella, you stay here to keep Annie company."

It seemed like forever before Jen returned, but at last the kitchen door opened and she appeared.

"You're right, Ella. Rosie's lame," she confirmed. "Her right knee is swollen.

Did she knock it against something?"

"Against the door," Ella told her, nodding. "Poor Rosie—she kicked it so hard that she forced it open."

"In that case, I'll give her a painkiller and something to help bring down the swelling, and then she'll need box-rest. With luck she won't have done any real damage."

Relieved, Ella turned to Annie. "Let's hope we get some good news about your mom, too," she said.

But when the phone rang an hour later and Mr. Brooks spoke to Annie, the news was bad. "Your mom just had an X-ray on her leg, and she's broken it in two places," he told her, sounding upset.

Shocked, Annie handed the phone to Ella.

"Tell Annie not to worry," Mr. Brooks insisted. "Her mom will be fine. The doctor will put her leg in a cast and she'll be on crutches for a while. But the leg will get better."

"I will," Ella promised.

"And please tell her that we'll be home by lunchtime," Mr. Brooks concluded. "Tell her everything is going to be fine."

Chapter Four

A Sad Decision

Gradually, the shock of Mrs. Brooks's accident wore off.

"It could have been worse," Jen told Annie. "And I'm sure the hospital is taking good care of your mom."

"It could happen to anyone," Caleb said. "I'm sure the emergency room is full of people who've slipped on the ice in weather like this."

"Does it hurt a lot when you break your leg?" Annie asked anxiously.

"Only until the doctors give you a painkiller," Jen explained. "A bit like the medicine I gave Rosie."

Talking things over, they waited patiently for Mr. Brooks to bring Mrs. Brooks home. Then, as soon as Annie heard their car, she said a hurried good-bye and ran to meet them.

A few minutes later, Joel's car appeared in the yard, and Ella rushed out to tell him what had happened.

"Whoa!" Joel cried after Ella's garbled account. "Who broke her leg—Rosie or Mrs. Brooks?"

"Mrs. Brooks. But Rosie's lame, too. I don't know what got into her, charging the fence like that."

"Twice!" Caleb added. He'd followed Ella out of the house with Holly.

"She's usually so good," Ella insisted. "But she seemed to think that if she jumped the fence, she could get back to Animal Magic."

"Hmm. I wonder why." Joel agreed that it was a mystery. "But listen, you two, we've got work to do. Dogs and cats to feed, small animal cages to clean out, a website to update...."

Ella was glad to be busy. Sunday afternoon was filled with chores, and when they'd finally finished at the rescue center, Ella and Joel paid a visit to Rosie in her stable. It was already getting dark, and there was no sign of Annie, Mrs. Brooks, or Mr. Brooks.

"We'll check the swelling on Rosie's leg without bothering the Brookses," Joel told Ella. "They probably want a quiet evening to get over the shock of the accident."

So they went into the stable to find Rosie standing in a corner, looking sad. She was keeping the weight off her injured leg and blowing softly through her nose.

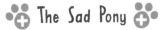

"There!" Ella said gently. She rubbed Rosie's neck while Joel ran his hand over the swollen knee.

"It feels warm," he reported. "The joint is inflamed, but she's not too uncomfortable when I touch it."

"There, Rosie," Ella breathed. "You hear that? You're going to be fine."

"I'll give her a thorough examination while I'm here," Joel decided. He looked for the light switch outside the stable door.

"Hello there, Joel." Mr. Brooks appeared around the side of the stables. "I was in the yard throwing dirt on the path. I heard noises."

"Hi, Mr. Brooks," Ella broke in. "Joel and Jen both think that Rosie's injury isn't too bad. She'll just need box-rest for a few days." She noticed that Annie's dad seemed to be frowning in the sudden glare of electric light.

"And how's Linda?" Joel asked.

Mr. Brooks sighed. "She's in bed. Her leg is in a cast up to the hip, and the painkiller really seems to have knocked her sideways. I'm hoping she'll get a good night's sleep."

"Let's hope so." Joel realized how tired Mr. Brooks must be. "Is it okay for me to give Rosie another dose of painkillers in her evening feed?"

"Yes, go ahead." Mr. Brooks watched Joel mix the medicine into Rosie's feed bucket. "Linda and I were talking on the drive back from the hospital. I said that I thought maybe she'd taken on too much. Three horses need a lot of care."

Instinctively, Ella put her arm around Rosie's neck.

"Give Rosie a chance to settle in," Joel suggested. "She won't be any trouble in the long run."

"I'm not so sure," Mr. Brooks argued. "Apparently she spent the entire day yesterday evening trying to kick her door down, and she was at it again early this morning. That's how Linda fell—she was hurrying out to see what the fuss was about."

"Shh!" Ella told Rosie as the pony raised her head and gave a shrill neigh.

There was a long pause before Mr. Brooks spoke again. "Linda and I are both surprised by what a handful Rosie can be."

"She's not usually…," Ella began to protest, but Joel gave her a warning glance.

"I'm sorry you feel that way, Jason. But you need to give it time."

Mr. Brooks seemed too upset to take any notice of Joel's reasoning. "There's not much point now that this has happened," he argued. "Linda's leg is in plaster, and it's going to be impossible for her to take care of three horses."

"Does Linda agree?" Joel asked.

No! Ella prayed she wasn't hearing this. She wanted to turn back time to before the accident, then play it through

again, this time with a happy ending
for Rosie.

"She sees the sense of what I'm
saying," Mr. Brooks replied. "And we
agree that Rosie doesn't seem to have
settled in as well as we'd hoped."

"I see," Joel said calmly. He stood
back to watch Rosie eat. "I think we
understand what you're telling us, don't
we, Ella?"

Ella bit her lip. *Please, Mr. Brooks, don't
do this!* she thought.

Mr. Brooks sighed. "I'm sorry, but
Rosie's too much for us to handle. So
I'm afraid we'll be sending her back to
Animal Magic—the sooner, the better."

Chapter Five

The Problem Pony

Both Annie and Ella were in tears over Rosie.

"Please persuade your dad to change his mind!" Ella begged. She'd run into the Brooks's house after Mr. Brooks had broken the news and found Annie sobbing in her bedroom. "Tell him you have to keep Rosie!"

"I've tried," Annie cried. She sat cross-legged on her bed, covering her face with her hands. "Honestly, Ella—

he won't listen."

"But your mom's accident wasn't Rosie's fault. It was the ice on the path that made her slip."

"I know!" Annie cried even harder. "Oh, Ella, this is all my fault. I shouldn't have blamed Rosie for Mom's accident. I only did it because I was so upset."

"No, it isn't your fault, either," Ella insisted. "But Annie, when your dad has calmed down, maybe you can talk to him again. Tell him I'll come twice a day to help with the mucking out. We can do this together."

Just then, Mr. Brooks passed Annie's bedroom door. "I know you mean well," he told Ella, "but even before Linda had her accident, we were beginning to think that Rosie wasn't happy here.

Now it seems that something—fate, or whatever you want to call it—is definitely telling us that we're not the right owners for her." He shook his head sadly, then walked on.

Annie sobbed quietly. "Dad means it, Ella. He won't change his mind."

Ella wiped her cheeks and sighed. "Okay, I'll tell Caleb."

"Tell him what?" Annie sniffed.

"To put Rosie's details back on the Animal Magic website. Starting tomorrow, we'll look for another home for her."

The silence after she spoke hung heavy in the air. They both thought of Rosie with her shaggy mane and mischievous eyes, her jaunty trot and playful habit of sniffing at your pocket for an apple or a carrot.

"I'm so sorry!" Annie said at last.

Ella nodded. "Me, too," she said as she left the room.

"We're still friends, aren't we?"

"Of course," Ella assured her sadly. "I'll see you, Annie. 'Bye."

"The thing that gets me," Ella told Caleb as she sat beside him in the reception area on Monday morning, "is that Mr. Brooks thinks Rosie's a problem, and she's not!"

"Rosie the problem pony," Caleb muttered. He looked through old files for her details, ready to put them back on the site.

"Rosie the perfect pony!" Ella insisted. "Make her sound good, Caleb. Tell everybody how cute she is."

"Hold it, you two." Jen came and looked over their shoulders. "Don't say anything that isn't true. We can't afford to mislead anyone."

"But what did she do wrong?" Ella refused to believe anything bad about the beautiful Rosie.

"Almost kicked the stable door down for a start," Jen pointed out. "And she tried to escape at least twice, didn't she? I'm not being mean, Ella, but you must admit she didn't settle in well at the Brookses."

"She did at first," Ella muttered. "Everything was okay until this weekend."

"Hmm, that's strange." Though Joel was busy admitting a new puppy, he joined in the conversation. "I wonder what went wrong all of a sudden. Anyway, Ella, let Caleb get going with the website entry. Why don't you come and help me with Baxter?"

Ella followed Joel into an examination room, where he took a puppy out of a pet carrier and placed him gently on the table. "Here's another unwanted Christmas present," he explained. "But not the kind you can take back to the store with the receipt for a refund."

Ella sighed. "And he's so handsome. Aren't you, Baxter?" She petted the long-haired, cream-colored puppy—a terrier type with big, pointed ears and a short tail.

Joel smiled. "He seems healthy, so I'll get him chipped and vaccinated, then we can take him into the kennels, settle him down, and give him a drink."

"I'll fill a water bowl," Ella offered, glad to have her mind taken off Rosie. But as she made her way toward the

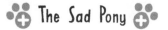

kennels, she saw her grandpa drive into the yard, and she did a rapid detour. "Hi, Grandpa. Guess who we've got back in our stables!"

"Hello, Ella. I have no idea." Grandpa grinned as he climbed out of his truck. "But I'm sure I'm about to find out!"

"Rosie!" Ella declared. "Joel brought her back from the Brookses place early this morning—before Annie was up so she didn't get too upset having to see Rosie leave. She's in here. Come and look."

Grandpa followed Ella into the clean, airy stables. They found Rosie in the nearest stall, her head poking over the door.

"Tell me honestly, Grandpa—does Rosie look like a problem pony to you?"

Newly brushed, with her
mane combed and her lively eyes
shining, the little Shetland looked
picture-book perfect.

Grandpa smiled. "No, she doesn't. But it's not what I think that matters. Now, Ella, come inside the house and share these warm croissants with me. I bought them at the supermarket just now."

"Yum!" If there was one thing that could drag Ella away from the animals, it was food. The croissants smelled good as she put them on a plate and her grandfather made himself coffee. In the background the TV was on, showing Tina Sanchez interviewing another one of her celebrity guests.

"Chat-chat-chitter-chat," Grandpa groaned, turning the TV off.

But Ella didn't hear him. She sat with her half-eaten croissant raised to her lips.

"What's wrong?" her grandpa asked.

"What? Um, nothing. Grandpa, do you mind if I go now? Joel asked me to help with Baxter the terrier. 'Bye!"

"No, I don't mind." Grandpa grinned as Ella sprinted off across the yard. Then he shook his head. "That's funny. She doesn't usually turn her nose up at warm croissants...."

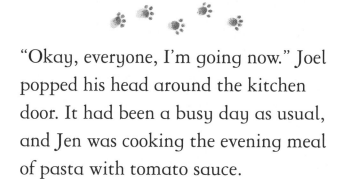

"Okay, everyone, I'm going now." Joel popped his head around the kitchen door. It had been a busy day as usual, and Jen was cooking the evening meal of pasta with tomato sauce.

"Stay to eat," Jen invited. "There's plenty of food."

Joel nodded. "If you're sure."

"Absolutely!" Jen insisted.

Ella set an extra place at the table. She hummed a tune she'd been repeating all day as she went about her chores in the kennels and the cat area, cleaning out the small animal cages and taking care of Rosie.

"There was one thing I wanted to do before I left," Joel remembered suddenly. "I was going to check on Rosie, so I'll quickly do it now."

"I'll come!" Ella volunteered in a flash.

"Caleb's still in the animal hospital. Tell him dinner will be ready in 10 minutes," Jen called after them.

"How's Rosie's leg?" Ella asked Joel as they hurried toward the stable.

Rosie whinnied a greeting. Her shaggy mane had fallen back over her twinkling eyes since Ella's morning grooming session.

"The swelling has going down nicely," Joel reported. He picked up the pony's feet one at a time to examine them closely. "No—nothing to worry about there."

"What are you looking for?" Ella asked, rubbing Rosie's neck.

Joel frowned. "I'm not sure. Something—anything that would make Rosie kick her door and take off across the field."

Ella nodded. "Yes, there must be a reason," she agreed. "Rosie doesn't normally act like that. She's usually so well-behaved!"

"And it wasn't anything in particular to do with the way Mrs. Brooks and Annie treated her?"

"No." Ella couldn't fault her neighbors. "They mucked her out properly, brushed her every day, gave her plenty of food and water."

"So why were you unhappy?" Joel asked quietly as he ran his hand along the pony's broad back.

Rosie shifted sideways, away from Joel and Ella.

"Hmm. Okay, we'll leave you in peace," Joel decided. "Come on, Ella. Close the door behind you. We'd better not keep Jen waiting."

The warm kitchen was full of delicious smells. Holly dozed on her bed in the corner.

"Did you remember to tell Caleb that

dinner was ready?" Jen asked.

"Oops! I'll go and get him," Ella said.

"No need!" Caleb announced, flinging open the door. He waved a sheet of paper under Ella's nose. "Look what I found!"

Ella gasped as she tried to grab the paper from him. "You snoop!"

"Honestly, Ella—only you could think up something as crazy as this!"

"Caleb, leave Ella alone," Jen told him.

He laid the paper flat on the table. "I knew from your face that you were up to something," he went on. "You've been doing it all day."

"Doing what?" Ella retorted.

"Smiling and singing—all that stuff you do when you've got a secret. Now I know what it is."

"So are you going to tell us?" Joel asked, carefully watching Ella's face, which was half-embarrassed, half-stubborn.

She shook her head and picked Holly up. "Let Caleb read it, since he thinks he's so clever."

So Caleb began to read. "'Dear Tina'— it's an email," he explained. "'I know how much you love horses and ponies because you said it on your show on Saturday.'"

"Tina who?" Joel interrupted.

"Tina Sanchez, the talk-show host," Caleb explained. "Listen to the rest. 'My name is Ella Harrison, and I live at an animal rescue center called Animal Magic. Our motto is, "Matching the perfect pet with the perfect owner." Well, we have a pony named Rosie who needs a new home.'" Caleb paused for breath.

"I don't understand," Jen muttered.

"She's had one of her brilliant ideas," Caleb cut in. "Listen. 'So I'd like you to have Rosie on your show so that lots of people can see her. Please say yes and help one poor pony find a wonderful new home. Thank you. From, Ella.'"

As Caleb finished reading, Jen stood in astonished silence.

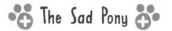

Ella frowned and held Holly tight,
ready to be teased again. Okay, so
maybe she'd been a bit hasty. Maybe
she should have talked to the others first
before she'd emailed Tina. Probably the
big TV star was way too busy to take
any notice....

"Magnificent!" Joel declared, beaming
at her. "That's a totally genius idea,
Ella. I hope it works!"

Chapter Six
Ella's Big Idea

Tuesday and Wednesday passed in another flurry of dog walks and animal admissions ... and no reply from the famous talk show host.

At dinnertime, a sad Annie came to visit Rosie.

"How's your mom?" Caleb asked as he pushed a wheelbarrow out of the stable.

"She's okay, but she's bored," Annie reported. "She can't do anything with her leg in a cast. How's Rosie?"

"Come and see," Ella said from inside the stable.

So Annie took a deep breath and reminded herself not to mope. She put on a smile and petted Rosie, gave her a carrot, and told her she was happy to see her. "How's her poor leg?" she asked.

"Much better," Ella told her. "Joel says that it'll be good as new in a day or two."

Rosie crunched the carrot contentedly, then nuzzled Annie's hand for more.

"All gone," Annie said with a smile. "You're so silly, Rosie!"

"Annie, I've got something to show you," Ella confided, pulling a crumpled copy of the email to Tina Sanchez out of her pocket. "Read this."

"Oh!" Annie gasped after she'd read it.

"We haven't gotten a reply yet, but what do you think?" Ella hoped Annie would approve. And she was glad she'd let her in on the plan.

There was a long silence as Annie's eyes filled with tears. "It's a cool idea—totally cool!" she whispered, backing out of the stables and leaving the yard just as Joel came out of the animal hospital with a visitor.

The two men headed straight for the stables where Ella was busy spreading clean straw. "Ella, this is Steve Cooper," Joel said. "Steve's a friend from college."

Ella looked up from her task. "Hi. Have you come to see Rosie?" she asked with a hopeful smile.

The visitor nodded. He was tall, like Joel, but heavier, with short, jet-black hair. He was wearing a leather jacket, jeans, and work boots. "But I don't want to adopt her," he added quickly.

"Oh." Ella's face fell. She felt like she was on a roller coaster of emotions—up, then down, up, and down again.

"No. I've asked Steve to examine Rosie," Joel explained. "He's a horse osteopath, and I want him to take a look at her back. Can you put her in a halter and hold her steady while he looks her over?"

As Ella fastened the halter, Steve gave the pony a quick pet, then rolled up his sleeves. He began to lay his hands along Rosie's spine, pressing gently and watching her reactions.

"Is there something wrong?" Ella asked Joel anxiously. She didn't even know what the long word Joel had used meant.

"We're not sure yet. But you know how Rosie's been acting oddly lately? Well, it occurred to me that there might be some hidden problem, and I noticed the other day that she didn't like me touching her back. That's when I thought of asking Steve to take a look. As an osteopath, he knows all about bones and back problems."

Ella nodded tensely. She held Rosie's halter while Steve examined her. The pony had all her attention on the visitor, with her ears flicked back and every nerve alert. Suddenly, as the osteopath's fingers hit a tender spot, she winced and pulled away.

"Steady!" Ella whispered, holding her firmly.

Steve concentrated on the problem spot, deep in the curve of her spine. "A-ha!" he said. "This explains everything."

"So Steve massaged Rosie's spine!" Ella told her mom on the phone. "He sort of kneaded it until everything clicked back into place!"

"Magic!" Mom said. "And this explains why Rosie wanted to get out of her stable—why she was kicking at the door?"

"Yes. Her back was hurting, so she needed to get out and run, and jump whatever got in her way—Steve says that's what horses do when they're in pain."

"And is she okay now?"

"She will be after another treatment."

"That's good news. And all thanks to Joel."

"Yes," Ella agreed. "We've found out what was wrong with Rosie, and now all we have to do is get Tina Sanchez to find her a home!"

Chapter Seven
An Exciting Phone Call

At nine o'clock that evening, Jen told
Ella that it was time to shut down the
computer. "Tina isn't going to reply to
your e-mail at this time of night," she
insisted. "She's probably already in bed,
getting her beauty sleep, which is what
you have to do, too."

"Okay," Ella grunted as she
reluctantly signed out.

"Never mind, it was worth trying."
Even Caleb had started being nice to her

over her so-called crazy idea. "If it had worked out, it would have been cool to have Rosie on TV."

Ella sighed. "There must be something else we can do."

"Yes—get to bed!" Jen smiled as the phone rang. "Lay your head on that nice soft pillow and snooze."

"I will," Ella agreed, pausing to pick up the phone as she headed for the stairs.

"Hello. May I speak to Ella Harrison?" a woman's voice asked.

"That's me," Ella stammered. She stared wide-eyed at Caleb and Jen.

"Ella, this is Fran Wood. I'm sorry to call so late. I'm a researcher on the Tina Sanchez Show."

Ella almost dropped the phone. What should she say? What should she do?

"Hello?" the voice said. "Ella, are you still there?"

"Yes. It's me. I'm here."

"We got your recent e-mail about the pony. I talked to Tina about it and we think your idea sounds interesting."

"Cool!" Ella gasped, as Caleb and Jen moved closer to the phone and Holly ran between everyone's legs.

"So I looked Rosie up on your website, and now I just want to check a few things with you," Fran said. "I need to ask you a few practical questions—is that okay?"

"Fine," Ella stammered.

"First, does the adult in charge of your rescue center know that you sent us the e-mail?"

Ella nodded, then realized Fran

couldn't see her. "I mean, yes. Jen's here right now."

"Good. I'll speak to her later. Second, has anyone else come forward to offer Rosie a home?"

"No. We haven't had a single inquiry."

"Excellent. Third, is Animal Magic down a narrow lane where our film crew would have difficulty with their large vans?"

"No. We're on Main Street in Crystal Park." Ella grew breathless as she tried to answer the quick-fire questions.

"And lastly, Tina wants us to be sure that there's nothing wrong with Rosie before we commit ourselves to giving her a slot on the Saturday show."

"What do you mean?" The question flustered Ella, and then she remembered what Jen had said about not misleading people. She had to tell the truth. "Well, actually, Rosie did have a problem at her previous owners' place."

"Oh." Fran's voice fell flat. "I'm sorry, Ella—that might put a stop to our featuring her on the show as we'd hoped."

"No, wait!" Ella cried. "The problem had to do with Rosie kicking her stable door and trying to run away, but we've just found out why she did it."

Standing close by, Jen was beginning to shake her head. Caleb, too, looked disappointed.

"Rosie hurt her back," Ella explained to Tina Sanchez's researcher. "The horse osti—ostepa…"

"Oste-o-path!" Caleb hissed.

"The horse osteopath came and fixed her. Now she's okay!" Gripping the phone and holding her breath, Ella waited for Fran to speak again.

"Hmm. You're sure about this?"

"Totally! Rosie's cured. She's not a problem anymore."

There was another pause, then Fran made up her mind. "That sounds like a great story, Ella. And Rosie certainly looks cute in her photo. I think this is something we could do after all."

"Really?" Ella gasped.

"Yes, really," Fran confirmed, her voice relaxing at last. "We'd definitely like to give Rosie a slot on our Saturday morning show."

"Tina Sanchez said yes!" Early next morning Ella rushed next door to

Annie's house. She blurted out her conversation with Fran Wood, then rode her bike up to her grandfather's garden center. "Grandpa, Rosie's going to be on the Tina Sanchez Show!"

Meanwhile, Caleb dashed off to tell his friend George Stevens, who lived on Three Oaks Road, and Miss Elliot on Arbor Court.

By nine o'clock, word had spread all over Crystal Park.

Ella was biking back to Animal Magic as a car marked with a film company's name drove up Main Street. "This way!" she yelled, standing at the gate.

Two men jumped out of the car, followed by a small, fair-haired woman.

"Hi—Ella?" she asked. "I'm Fran. Nice to meet you."

As the men started to take a look around the yard, Caleb showed up, too. He and Ella proudly showed Fran around the center.

"We've been open for almost two years," Caleb explained. "Dad built the stables last year. This is where we keep Rosie."

"I think Steve is in here with Joel," Ella announced as she opened the door and led the visitor in. "Steve is the horse osteopath."

"Hi, Ella. I've finished Rosie's second treatment." Steve petted the little pony's nose, then introduced himself to Fran. "Joel has told me all about the slot on Tina's show. You can take it from me that this little pony won't have any more back problems. She's ready to go to a nice new home."

Rosie raised her head and neighed as if she was agreeing with him.

Fran smiled. "Now then, Rosie, you have to be on your best behavior tomorrow morning when Tina gets here."

"She will be," Ella promised. Then she gave a nervous cough. "Um, what's Tina like?" she asked, thinking of the sleek, glamorous woman in bright, tailored suits who appeared on the TV screen.

"Scary!" Fran joked. "No, actually she's really nice and friendly. So don't be nervous. Maybe you'd like to prepare a speech about Rosie—her history, what's happened to her lately, what kind of home you're looking for, that kind of thing."

"A speech?" Ella stammered.

"Yes. Something nice and short. You'll be facing the camera with Rosie standing beside you. Our technical guys will set up lights and microphones here in the stable. After your introduction to Rosie, Tina will ask you a few questions."

"Questions?" Ella gasped. She was beginning to feel a little queasy.

"Yes, just a friendly chat," Fran assured her. She stood to the side as one of the crew came in to check the lighting. "Okay, that's all for now," she told Ella. "I'll give you a call if there's anything else I need to know."

Chapter Eight
Rosie's Big Day

At seven o'clock on Friday morning, Ella laid out her horse combs and brushes, shampoo, sprays, buckets, and hoof oil. "Rosie, this is your big day," she said.

Outside it was dark, damp, and cold—the start of a typical January day. Inside the stables the electric light cast a yellow glow.

Rosie sniffed the bucket filled with warm water and lavender shampoo, sighing as Ella gently sponged her

back and withers.

"I've got a special detangler for your mane to make it silky smooth," Ella told her. "You're going to smell wonderful and look sooo beautiful for the camera!"

It was hard work to groom Rosie to the point where she shone and sparkled, but at last Ella stood back to admire her. Looking at her watch, she saw it was quarter to nine.

"Ready?" Caleb asked, poking his head around the door. "The director and the camera and sound guys are already here. They're in the kitchen having coffee with Jen and Joel."

"Is Tina here yet?" Ella asked. She realized she had less than 15 minutes to get changed and spruced up.

"She's on her way with Fran." Caleb stared at Ella's splashed sweatshirt and bedraggled hair. "Better get a move on," he warned.

Ella was in her bedroom, dressed in fresh jeans and her favorite red sweatshirt, drying her hair when she looked out the window and saw a silver car pull into the yard.

She watched as a tall, slim woman with neatly cut blond hair stepped out of the car into the chilly air. She was wearing a dark blue jacket and matching pants, and looked very smart.

"Ella, Tina's here!" Caleb called from the foot of the stairs.

So she dashed down, rehearsing her speech word for word and trembling from top to toe.

Rosie is a five-year-old Shetland pony.... *She's fully schooled and loves children.... We're looking for a home with other ponies....*

"Hello—you must be Ella," Tina said as Ella caught up with her and Fran.

Ella felt her face turn red. Tina Sanchez was everything a TV star should be— glossy and smiley, with perfect hair and make-up. She mumbled hello and shuffled along, panicking in case she forgot her speech and let Rosie down.

"Everything's set up," Fran told Tina as she guided her toward the stables.

"You did a good job in your e-mail." Tina smiled at Ella. "I wish I'd been as smart when I was your age."

"Thanks," Ella muttered.

Tina went on chatting inside the stables as a make-up girl fussed and a sound man did a check. "So you love animals?" she asked Ella.

Ella nodded. *Rosie is a five-year-old Shetland pony.... She's fully schooled....*

"Now tell us, Ella, what's special about Rosie?" Tina asked with a warm, encouraging smile.

It happened so fast that Ella didn't even know the camera was pointing at her.

"Rosie's clever," she answered. "She knows exactly what you're saying, especially if you're talking about her."

At that second, Rosie appeared at her stall door. She pushed it open and poked her head between Ella and their famous guest.

"See, she knows!" Ella smiled. "She can be very playful, but she's never really naughty. And she loves getting lots of attention."

"And how come Rosie needs a new home?" Tina asked.

"Oh, that's because she had a problem," Ella explained in a rush.

"A problem pony?" Tina interrupted. "I guess that makes it especially hard to find a new home for her?"

"It could, but we hope not. When she lived at her last place, she used to kick the stable door and try to run away." Suddenly, Ella noticed that the camera light was on and pointing in her direction. *Oh, no!* she thought. *I've ruined it for Rosie. Now no one will want her.* And she stopped dead.

Tina Sanchez continued smiling at the camera. "But luckily, that's not the end of Rosie's story," she told the viewers. "Here we are with a beautiful little Shetland who had a couple of behavioral problems that seemed to rule her out for adoption. But Ella, why don't you tell everyone what happened next."

Ella quickly pulled herself together.
Don't be nervous, she told herself.
*Concentrate on Rosie and do your very best
for her.* "We found out what was wrong
soon after she came back here," she
explained. "It turned out Rosie had a
bad back—the horse osteopath said it
was a trapped nerve that was hurting
and making her act up."

"Really?" Tina interrupted. "That's interesting. What looked like naughtiness turned out to be a physical problem after all."

That was it exactly! Ella nodded eagerly. "Steve cured it, and now Rosie's a perfect pony again!"

"That's wonderful, Ella—it really is." As Rosie nudged the glamorous visitor with her nose, Tina wrapped up the interview. "We're looking for a real fairy-tale ending," she explained to the camera. "Animal Magic is a fabulous rescue center set up to match the perfect pet with the perfect owner. When Ella e-mailed us an emergency appeal for help, we decided it was time for the Tina Sanchez Show to step in."

Rosie snuggled up to Tina and seemed

to nod. Her bright eyes sparkled, and her shiny mane shone like silk.

Tina's smile broadened. "So if anyone watching already has a pony who needs a friend and stable mate, we'd like you to contact Animal Magic directly. Details are on your screen right now."

Chapter Nine

TV Stars!

At nine o'clock next morning Ella, Caleb, Jen, and Joel were glued to the TV screen.

"Tina said we get the first slot on the Saturday show," Caleb reminded them.

"I can't bear to look!" Ella sighed, hugging Holly and hoping that she didn't come across as a total goofball.

"Ten—nine—eight—seven...," Joel counted down as the Tina Sanchez signature tune began.

✿ TV Stars! ✿

"Good morning!" Tina greeted her viewers warmly from the studio. "Today we're starting with a feel-good story about Rosie the problem pony who turns out not to be such a problem after all!"

Caleb nudged Ella and grinned at her. Jen turned up the volume and listened intently.

"Yesterday I spent the day at a wonderful rescue center called Animal Magic," Tina went on as the scene changed to their own yard.

"It's us—we're on TV!" Caleb cried. "Look, there's our house!"

"And the kennels and the cat area!" Ella watched as the camera panned around toward the stables. "We're actually on TV—wow!"

"Animal Magic is a very special

place—and I'm here to meet
a wonderful new friend," Tina
explained, her blond hair shining on
the screen.

The camera swung away from her and
captured Ella leading the way into the
stables.

"It's you!" Caleb yelled.

"Shh! I know it's me." Ella got ready
to cringe with embarrassment.

"And Rosie," Jen added, as for the first time the little pony appeared and posed for the camera.

"Meet Rosie," Tina said, "and her caregiver, Ella Harrison. Now tell us, Ella, what's so special about Rosie?"

"Rosie's clever," Ella explained to her guest. Her red sweatshirt made her look bright and cheerful. Her long hair was neatly tied back, with only a wisp or two escaping from her ponytail. "She knows exactly what you're saying, especially if you're talking about her...."

"Amazing!" Joel grinned as Tina ended the segment and took the viewers back to the Saturday morning studio. "You're a TV natural," he told Ella.

"That was cool," Caleb agreed. "I'd definitely want to adopt Rosie after watching that."

Ella sighed happily. "How cute did Rosie look!"

"And now we all have to get over to the reception area in double quick time," Joel told them. "With luck, viewers will be calling us already."

So they turned off the TV and hurried across the yard to find the Animal Magic phone red hot with callers.

"I'm interested in your Shetland pony," one viewer of Tina's show explained to Jen. "Can you tell me again how old Rosie is?"

Or, "Rosie is the ideal pony for my six-year-old daughter. She looks like such fun!"

Or, "I fell in love with the pony on the Tina Sanchez Show. Can I drive over with my mom to see her?"

For a full hour, the phone kept ringing.

"We have to write down names and phone numbers," said Jen. From the start, she was the organized one. "Caleb, here's the appointment book. Can you make a note of times when people want to come?"

"How old is your daughter?" Joel asked one eager caller. "No, I'm afraid three's a little too young. Wait a year or two, then take another look at our website. We'll always have ponies who need new homes. Thank you for calling. Good-bye."

"How many people definitely want to come and see Rosie?" Ella asked Caleb after another hour had passed.

Together they checked the appointment book and counted eight definite appointments.

"The first people say they can get here by 11 this morning," Caleb said.

"I see Animal Magic is a hive of activity, as expected." Grandpa arrived in the reception area with a broad smile. "Where's my TV star granddaughter?"

Ella grinned back. "Was it okay?"

"Ella, I was so proud, I almost burst!"

"Hi, Jimmy," Joel took a break between phone calls. "And hi, Annie. Did you see Ella on television?"

Annie had just arrived in the doorway. "You were great," she told Ella with a smile. "Have you had many phone calls?"

"So many!" Ella replied. "The TV idea worked really well."

"So Rosie won't be here much longer?" Annie seemed to hover uneasily by the door. "Mom's here with me. Do you mind if we go and see her one last time?"

"I'll come, too." Quickly Ella left the desk and ran to join Annie and Mrs. Brooks. Mrs. Brooks looked pale and leaned heavily on her crutches to cross the yard.

"This is the hard part," Mrs. Brooks sighed as they went into the stables. "I know that we've done the right thing, but I'm still so fond of little Rosie."

"I know. I hate saying good-bye to our animals," Ella admitted. "I always wish they could stay."

"But we've still got Buttercup and Chance." Mrs. Brooks tried to look on the bright side.

"And you promise you won't let Rosie go to just anyone?" Annie pleaded, softly rubbing Rosie's nose.

"I totally promise!" Ella replied. "She'll go to the best place because she deserves it. Don't you, Rosie?"

The bright little Shetland gave a short neigh, then went back to munching hay from her net. Don't bother me while I'm eating, she seemed to say. Come back later when I'm ready for visitors!

An hour later, Ella was back in the stables for the first appointment. "Come and meet Emma and her mom," she told Rosie, leading her out into the yard.

"Ahh!" Emma Benson squealed the moment Rosie trotted into view. "She's beautiful. I want her, Mom—please, please, please!"

Rosie snorted and tossed her head.

I agree, Ella thought. *Emma's voice is too screechy, and she shouldn't stamp her feet like that.*

Next on the appointment list came Jake Wade with his father, John. Jake was quiet and calm, and Rosie seemed to like him. But he was too tall to ride her, so his dad said no thank you.

Then there was nervous Gracie Marks with her older sister, Paige. Gracie burst into tears when Rosie nudged her pocket, asking for a treat.

Then came twin girls, Amy and Lucy, who wanted to share Rosie and argued right away over who would have the first ride.

By midday, Ella had trotted Rosie out into the yard half a dozen times without success.

"Maybe the TV thing wasn't such a good idea after all," she sighed.

Fed-up little Rosie seemed to agree, searching Ella's pocket for a carrot.

But then Caleb brought over a couple named Mr. and Mrs. Baker and their daughter, Martha. "They live in the next town, 20 miles away," he said.

"I'm sorry we couldn't get here earlier," Mrs. Baker told Ella. "We had an appointment with our farrier. He came to shoe my husband's horse, Dexter, and it was too late to change his time."

"What do you think of Rosie?" Mr. Baker asked Martha. "Do you like her?"

"She's pretty," Martha said. "She looks a little like Daisy."

"Daisy was Martha's last pony," her mother explained. "Sadly, Daisy was very old and died last fall. We've been looking around for another Shetland ever since."

All this time Rosie had stood quietly beside Ella, but now she took a step forward and began to nudge Martha's arm in a let-me-be-your-friend way.

"And friendly." Martha smiled. "Look, Dad—she likes me!"

"I think she does," Mr. Baker agreed. "And we all like her, don't we?"

Ella stood well back, letting Rosie do her stuff. *Sooo smart!* she thought.

"So should we give her a home?" Mrs. Baker asked. "Should we put her in the stable next to Dexter and let you two ride out together? What do you say?"

Martha put her arm around Rosie's neck. "Yes, please!" she sighed.

And Rosie nodded so that her mane fell forward, and she peeked at Ella with a mischievous gleam in her eye.

Chapter Ten
Rosie's New Home

"So this is Rosie's last day in Crystal Park?" Dad led Mom, Caleb, and Ella across the yard to the stables.

It was Tuesday, and Mom and Dad were back from their vacation looking tanned and relaxed. Their bulging suitcases were still in the car. Inside the house, Joel was saying good-bye to Jen, ready to head back to Australia.

"It's Rosie's very last morning," Ella said. "The Bakers are bringing their

horsebox this afternoon and driving Rosie to their place."

"Which we went to and checked out with Jen," Caleb explained. "They live in a massive house with a bunch of stables and a big paddock. It's like a luxury hotel for horses!"

"And they're really nice people." Now that the day had come, Ella was more excited than sad. "Martha loves ponies!"

"As much as you?" her dad asked with a smile. He held the stable door open while Ella, Caleb, and Mom went in.

"No one loves ponies as much as Ella!" Caleb cried. "That would be impossible."

"Hey, you hear that, Rosie?" Ella sighed, putting her arm around the pony's neck. "They're making fun of me and saying I'm crazy about you!"

Rosie nudged Ella's cheek with her nose.

"Well, you definitely did a good job of finding a new home for this little girl," Mom told Ella. "I don't think anyone could have tried harder or had a better idea than getting her on the Tina Sanchez Show!"

Ella beamed at her mom and dad. "Even Annie and Mrs. Brooks are happy in the end. The Bakers are happy. Rosie's happy. I'm happy!"

"And it was wonderful publicity for Animal Magic," Mom added, smiling at Ella.

"Which can't be bad," her dad added. He looked around the stables at three smiling faces. "I'm glad to be back," he told them all. "Florida was great, but there's honestly and truly no better place to come back to than Animal Magic Rescue Center!"